POULTRYGEIST

POULTRYGEIST

POULTRYGEIST

Eric Geron

illustrated by Pete Oswald

CANDLEWICK PRESS

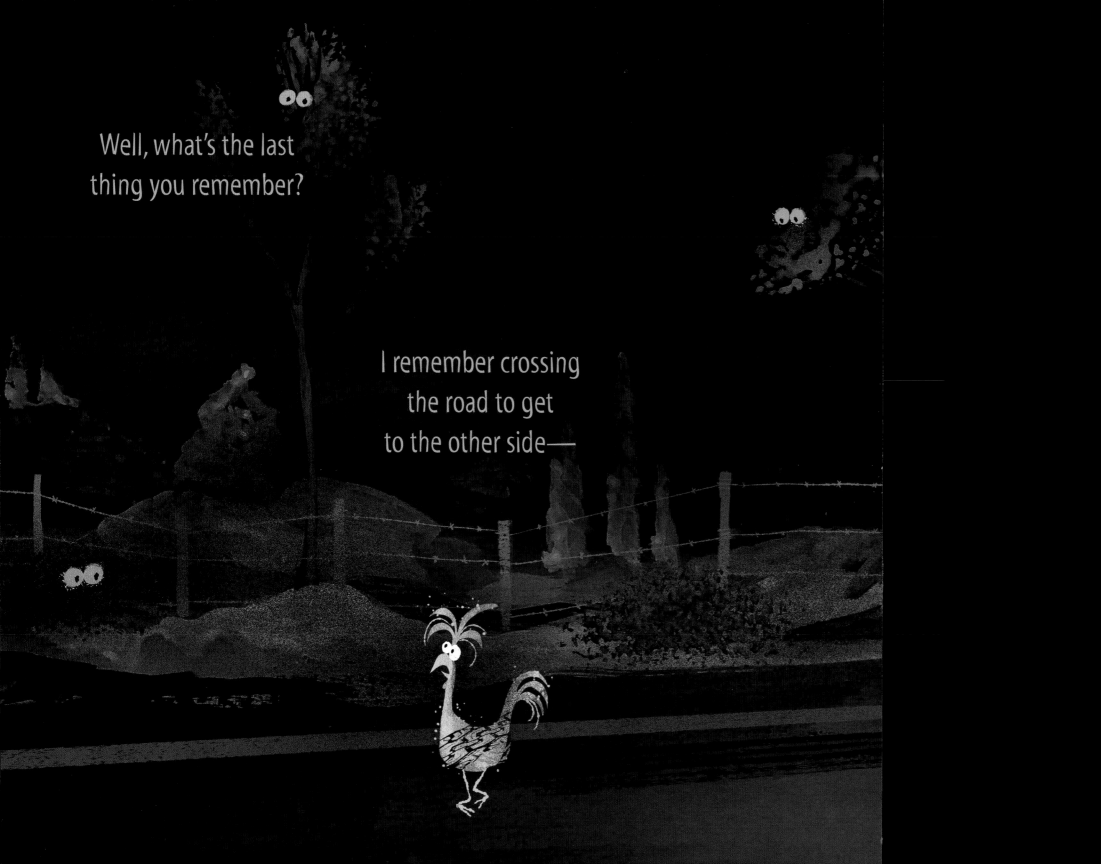

Well, what's the last
thing you remember?

I remember crossing
the road to get
to the other side—

Isn't that what I said?

You mean
THE OTHER SIDE.

Anyway, I remember crossing the road to
get to THE OTHER SIDE, like I always do ...

Beeeak!

You mean I'm . . .

I'm . . . ?

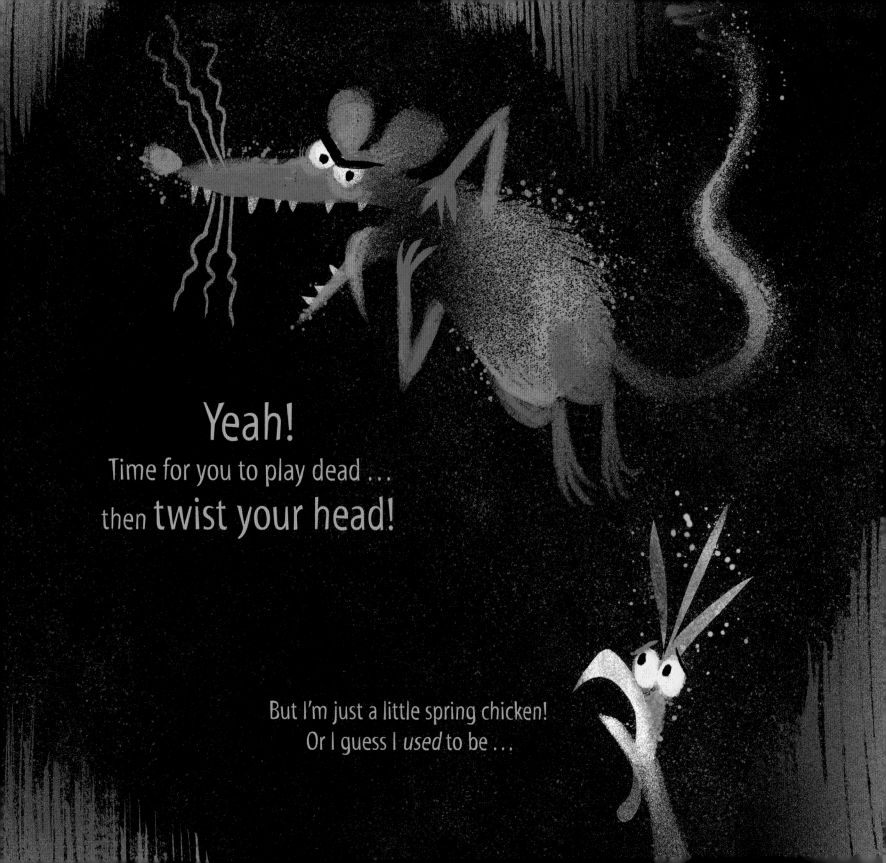

Yeah!
Time for you to play dead ...
then twist your head!

But I'm just a little spring chicken!
Or I guess I *used* to be ...

No. Your goal,
now that you're a ghoul,
is to turn someone's
sunny side up . . . into
**sunny side
down.**

But I don't want to haunt anyone,
especially not innocent readers who are just trying
to enjoy a nice story about an unlucky chicken.

Ghosts of a feather **haunt** together!

Show a little **pluck,** Cluck!

Hatch a scheme to get a **scream!**

I may be a ghost, but I will not haunt anyone. **Nothing** you do or say can ever change that.

And besides …

Oh, well. Good riddance.

For my mother hen, Marie
EG

For Kirsten
PO

First edition 2021

Library of Congress Catalog Card Number pending
ISBN 978-1-5362-1050-7

21 22 23 24 25 26 APS 10 9 8 7 6 5 4 3 2 1

Printed in Humen, Dongguan, China

This book was typeset in Myriad Std.
The illustrations were created digitally.

No chickens were harmed in the making of this book.

Candlewick Press
99 Dover Street
Somerville, Massachusetts 02144

www.candlewick.com